KAYA'S FARM
The Koi

Bela Sharma Bratch

BELA SHARMA BRATCH

Kaya's Farm
Copyright © 2022 by Bela Sharma Bratch
Illustrated by Jupiter's Muse

All rights reserved. No part of this publication may be reproduced, distributed, or transmitted in any form or by any means, including photocopying, recording, or other electronic or mechanical methods, without the prior written permission of the author, except in the case of brief quotations embodied in critical reviews and certain other non-commercial uses permitted by copyright law.

Tellwell Talent
www.tellwell.ca

ISBN
978-0-2288-7525-3 (Paperback)

For my children, Kaya, Niam and Avaani, who wholeheartedly share my love of animals and storytelling.

One late-winter morning, when Kaya was eleven years old, she heard Avaani call out, "Hey Niam, it looks like the snow is melting."

"Yahoo, I can't wait until the warm spring weather. I am so excited to see the koi wake up from its winter nap," exclaimed Niam.

"Kaya, please tell us the story of the koi again," the five-year-old twins asked in unison.

Kaya laughed at their excitement. "Of course, but you must settle down. Mommy and Daddy have shared the story of the koi with me every spring since I was a little girl, so I know it by heart."

The twins and Kaya cuddled up on the couch in the sunroom. They were surrounded by their dogs, Jersey, the Border Collie, and Bonnie, the Australian Shepherd. Their barn cats Lentil, Maple and Popo were curled up on the cushions.

Kaya began the story:
"A long time ago, a wealthy family lived on our farm property. There was a mom and a dad and several children. The mom and dad built multiple houses on the property for their children and employees to live in. Guests would arrive in stretch limousines and enjoy lavish tea parties by the pond."

"The family employed a gardener who lived in one of the houses. His background was Japanese, and because of this influence, he created beautiful Japanese-style rock gardens on the property. In one of the rock gardens, at the front of the house, there was a beautiful waterfall and miniature pond. Within that pond lived multiple koi. The koi are a beautiful fish."

"They can grow between two to three feet long, and they come in many colours. The koi in the pond were multicoloured – orange, white, brown and marbled. In Japan, the koi fish are considered to be symbols of good luck, wealth and perseverance." Kaya paused, waiting for the question that always came at this point in the story.

"Does that mean that the koi fish is hardworking and very, very rich?" giggled Avaani.

Kaya smiled and continued, "What it means is that the koi fish would bring people good luck. The koi fish would wish for the people to be hardworking and surrounded by not only a wealth of money, but also the wealth of a loving family and community. The koi fish are also known to live for a very long time. There are tales of koi that live to the ripe old age of 200 years. Isn't that amazing?"

"Wow, that's really old," exclaimed Niam. He added, "They must be very wise and smart."

"Wow, they must be all wrinkly," declared Avaani, "and maybe a bit smelly."

Kaya grinned and responded, "Yes, Niam, that certainly is old, and I am sure the koi are very wise. Avaani, I don't believe the koi become wrinkly. When they are old, they continue to look smooth and beautiful. And, I have not been close enough to the koi to tell if they smell. Now, let's continue with the story of our koi. The gardener taking care of the koi decided to move the koi from the front gardens' miniature pond to the newly built large pond at the bottom of the hill. From what I understand, the koi were producing lots of babies or offspring which are referred to as 'fry.'" Kaya paused the story once again, as she knew what would happen next.

Just like clockwork, the twins rolled around on the floor laughing and singing "French fries, French fries, there are French fries swimming in the pond."

Kaya waited patiently for the twins to settle down before continuing her story. "The gardener collected the koi carefully with a large net and placed them in a large bucket and carried them to the pond. The koi were very happy, as the pond was the size of a football field and over fifteen feet deep. They had plenty of room to swim and sun themselves in the warm weather. And when winter came, the koi could swim deep below the surface and hibernate. This means that the koi would remain nearly motionless to conserve their energy. This is how they could survive the cold winter months."

The twins simultaneously jumped off the couch and lay still on the floor, imitating the motionless koi hibernating at the bottom of the pond.

"Is this how the koi hibernate, Kaya?" the twins yelled out.

Kaya laughed and answered, "Yes, that is exactly how they lay still."

Kaya continued, "When Mommy and Daddy moved to the property many years ago, there were six beautiful koi swimming in the pond. They were over two feet long and multicoloured, mostly a bright iridescent orange colour with white and brown spots.

When I was little, I would run down to the pond with Mommy, Daddy, Jersey and our old dog Emily. I was hoping to see the koi swimming in the pond after waking up from their long winter nap. I would be so excited when I saw them surface. Emily, Jersey and I would sit by the pond and watch over them as they glided around in circles and made criss-cross designs. Our cats, Lentil and Corey – Corey, who has since passed, was Popo's and Maple's mother – would often join us frolicking at the water's edge trying to catch the koi, which, luckily for the koi, the cats never could."

"It's really a magical feeling to see them swim. It makes your heart feel so good that they survived the long cold winter. Over the years, sadly, the koi dwindled down and only one remains. Mommy and Daddy believe this koi is between fifty to sixty years old. Now I get to share this incredible experience with the two of you."

"We can't wait, we can't wait," chimed the twins.

Soon, all the snow disappeared, and the warm spring arrived. Kaya, Niam and Avaani ran down the hill to the pond. Jersey and Bonnie chased after them. The children knew the hiding places of the koi. They knew that the koi loved to stretch itself out in the sunshine. Each morning the children were filled with excitement, hoping that today was the day the koi would show itself. They called out "Good morning" to the singing red-winged blackbirds, the chirping sparrows and the drumming woodpeckers as they searched for the koi amongst the dried bulrushes and cattails.

They saw schools of bass fish swimming in the pond. They heard the chorus of the spring peepers. They knew they had to be patient. The koi would show itself when it was ready. They took turns visiting the pond at various times during the day. They observed that the globeflowers tucked in at the edge of the pond were beginning to bloom. Their golden yellow buds opened toward the rays of the sun. The children picnicked by the pond. They laid out their sandwiches, chips and drinks on their red and white checkered picnic blanket, leaving space for Lentil, Maple and Popo to stretch out. They brought extra treats for Jersey and Bonnie who sat patiently nearby.

They played in the field adjacent to the hillside. They climbed the trees overlooking the cow pasture. They waited faithfully. At last, the day arrived. Swimming gracefully out of the cover of the dried bulrushes into the rays of the sun, with its long flowing fin and spectacular bright golden orange colour, was the koi in all its glory. Kaya, Niam and Avaani were ecstatic to see the beautiful koi floating freely in its pond, ready for another ageless summer.

About the Author:

Bela lives on a farm in Carlisle, Ontario with her husband and three children. They are surrounded by nature and by their adventurous pets. After the birth of their daughter Kaya, Bela would regale Kaya with stories of their pets' adventures while living on "Kaya's Farm". There were many stories to tell. Bela, wanting to share these stories, began writing a series about her family and their pets living on "Kaya's Farm". What makes these stories extra special is that they are real. The people and animals exist, the events have truly occurred, and the animals' experiences are interpreted through Bela's eyes.

The Koi introduces many new characters: Niam and Avaani, our ancient koi, our Australian Shepherd Bonnie, and Corey's kittens, Maple and Popo. Below are pictures of Emily in our pond with the original six koi, circa 1999, Corey with her kittens, Maple and Popo, Bonnie with Emily and Lentil, and a picture taken in the spring of 2021 of our last surviving koi.

Printed in the USA
CPSIA information can be obtained
at www.ICGtesting.com
LVHW070927070924
790422LV00022B/122